This
Treasure Cove Story
belongs to

RATATOUILLE

A CENTUM BOOK 978-1-910917-81-7
Published in Great Britain by Centum Books Ltd.
This edition published 2020.

1 3 5 7 9 10 8 6 4 2

Centum Books Ltd, 20 Devon Square, Newton Abbot, Devon, TQ12 2HR, UK.
9/10 Fenian St, Dublin 2, D02 RX24, Ireland.

www.centumbooksltd.co.uk | books@centumbooksltd.co.uk
CENTUM BOOKS Limited Reg. No. 07641486.

A CIP catalogue record for this book is available
from the British Library.

Printed in China.

A Treasure Cove Story

Disney · PIXAR

RATATOUILLE
(rat·a·too·ee)

MENU

Written by
Victoria Saxon

Illustrated by
**Scott Tilley
& Jean-Paul Orpiñas**

Designed by
Tony Fejeran

This is
the story
of Remy,
a little rat
with
BIG
dreams.

Remy wasn't like all the other rats. For one thing, he had an extraordinary sense of

SMELL.

He also had a taste for finer food.

And *THAT* is why Remy dreamed of being...
a *CHEF!*

But Django,
Remy's father,
had another
job for him...

...poison checker. The compost heap was
where the rats got all their food. Remy had the
important job of sorting the safe garbage from the
bad garbage. This was **NOT** part of his dream.

One day,
the rats had to flee
their home. A **HUMAN**
had discovered them!
As the human chased them,
the rats ran to their
ESCAPE boats and
floated into
the sewers.

Remy got separated from the others
and ended up near a fancy French
restaurant in
PARIS.

The restaurant used to belong to Remy's idol, the late and great chef, Auguste Gusteau. Now Gusteau popped up in Remy's

IMAGINATION.

Then – whoops!

Remy fell from
the skylight into
the kitchen.

The restaurant
was an **EXCITING**
place for Remy, but it was
SCARY too.

In the kitchen, Remy cooked a pot of soup to replace what the garbage boy had spilled. The garbage boy was named Linguini. After that, Linguini and Remy became friends. *AND* they were a secret cooking team.

SHHHH!

Meanwhile, Django and the rest of the rat colony made a new home in the dark, wet sewers under Paris. Things weren't the same without Remy. Django kept hoping he would find his son one day.

But Remy was happy. He did miss his family, but he had found his place in the world. Working together, Linguini and Remy made great food, even though Remy had to stay hidden. The human chefs did not want a rat in their kitchen!

Once, after cooking a wonderful meal, the chefs celebrated in the kitchen. Remy celebrated too, in the back alley, where…

…he found his brother **EMILE!**

Emile took Remy **HOME**
to the rats' new colony
in the sewer.

Of course, Django was **HAPPY** to see Remy again!

But Remy didn't feel as if he belonged with the rats anymore. He didn't want to go back to smelling garbage.

'I have friends, a place to live, work that
I love,' Remy tried to explain to his dad.
'I'll come back often,' he said. But
for now he had to return to his
new home and the restaurant.
Remy's dad didn't understand.

Remy went back to being a little chef. Meanwhile, Linguini was falling in **LOVE**!

Soon Linguini found out that he was the owner of the restaurant! And the restaurant was becoming very famous. Linguini enjoyed the attention.

Linguini decided he didn't need Remy anymore. They **ARGUED.**

Remy felt very
SAD
and
ALONE.

Who was his
family now?

But Linguini needed **HELP.**

He had to cook a special dinner for a special guest. And Linguini told Remy he was **SORRY.** **UH-OH!** The other chefs didn't like rats, so they left.

Django saw
Linguini being kind
to Remy.
He asked everyone
in the rat colony to
pitch in to help make
the special dinner.
All the rats became
little chefs!

With the rats' help,
the meal was a success.
The SPECIAL dish was
ratatouille!

The rats also helped Remy **CHASE** away the health inspector…

…who still **CLOSED** the restaurant for having rats.

That gave Remy and his friends an idea. They opened a **NEW** one!

And Remy's colony ate at the restaurant, too – enjoying all the fine food they could ever want.

Treasure Cove Stories

Please contact Centum Books to receive the full list of titles in the *Treasure Cove Stories* series.
books@centumbooksltd.co.uk

Classic favourites

1 Three Little Pigs
2 Snow White and
the Seven Dwarfs
3 The Fox and the Hound
- Hide-and-Seek
4 Dumbo
5 Cinderella
6 Cinderella's Friends
7 Alice in Wonderland
8 Mad Hatter's Tea Party
from Alice in Wonderland
9 Mickey Mouse and
his Spaceship
10 Peter Pan
11 Pinocchio
12 Mickey and the Beanstalk
13 Sleeping Beauty
and the Good Fairies
14 The Lucky Puppy
15 Chicken Little
16 The Incredibles
17 Coco
18 Winnie the Pooh and Tigger
19 The Sword in the Stone
20 Mary Poppins
21 The Jungle Book
22 The Aristocats
23 Lady and the Tramp
24 Bambi
25 Bambi - Friends of the Forest

Recently published

50 Frozen
51 Cinderella is my Babysitter
52 Beauty and the Beast
- I am the Beast
53 Blaze and the Monster Machines
- Mighty Monster Machines
54 Blaze and the Monster Machines
- Dino Parade!
55 Teenage Mutant Ninja Turtles
- Follow the Ninja!

56 I am a Princess
57 The Big Book of Paw Patrol
58 Paw Patrol
- Adventures with Grandpa!
59 Paw Patrol - Pirate Pups!
60 Trolls
61 Trolls Holiday
62 The Secret Life of Pets
63 Zootropolis
64 Ariel is my Babysitter
65 Tiana is my Babysitter
66 Belle is my Babysitter
67 Paw Patrol
- Itty-Bitty Kitty Rescue
68 Moana
69 Nella the Princess Knight
- My Heart is Bright!
70 Guardians of the Galaxy
71 Captain America
- High-Stakes Heist!
72 Ant-Man
73 The Mighty Avengers
74 The Mighty Avengers
- Lights Out!
75 The Incredible Hulk
76 Shimmer & Shine
- Wish Upon a Sleepover
77 Shimmer & Shine - Backyard Ballet
78 Paw Patrol - All-Star Pups!
79 Teenage Mutant Ninja Turtles
- Really Spaced Out!
80 I am Ariel
81 Madagascar
82 Jasmine is my Babysitter
83 How to Train your Dragon
84 Shrek
85 Puss in Boots
86 Kung Fu Panda
87 Beauty and the Beast - I am Belle
88 The Lion Guard
- The Imaginary Okapi
89 Thor - Thunder Strike!
90 Guardians of the Galaxy
- Rocket to the Rescue!
91 Nella the Princess Knight
- Nella and the Dragon
92 Shimmer & Shine
- Treasure Twins!

93 Olaf's Frozen Adventure
94 Black Panther
95 Trolls
- Branch's Bunker Birthday
96 Trolls - Poppy's Party
97 The Ugly Duckling
98 Cars - Look Out for Mater!
99 101 Dalmatians
100 The Sorcerer's Apprentice
101 Tangled
102 Avengers
- The Threat of Thanos
103 Puppy Dog Pals
- Don't Rain on my Pug-Rade
104 Jurassic Park
105 The Mighty Thor
106 Doctor Strange

Latest publications

107 Captain Marvel
108 The Invincible Iron Man
109 Black Panther
- Warriors of Wakanda
110 The Big Freeze
111 Ratatouille
112 Aladdin
113 Aladdin - I am the Genie
114 Seven Dwarfs Find a House
115 Toy Story
116 Toy Story 4
117 Paw Patrol - Jurassic Bark!
118 Paw Patrol
- Mighty Pup Power!
119 Shimmer & Shine
- Pet Talent Show!
120 SpongeBob SquarePants
- Krabby Patty Caper
121 The Lion King - I am Simba
122 Winnie the Pooh
- The Honey Tree
123 Frozen II
124 Baby Shark and the
Colours of the Ocean
125 Baby Shark and
the Police Sharks!
126 Trolls World Tour

Book list may be subject to change.